I AM A WARRIOR GODDESS

BY JENNIFER ADAMS
ILLUSTRATED BY CARME LEMNISCATES

BOULDER, COLORADO

I am a warrior goddess.

Each day
I greet the sun

and the earth

and the wind.

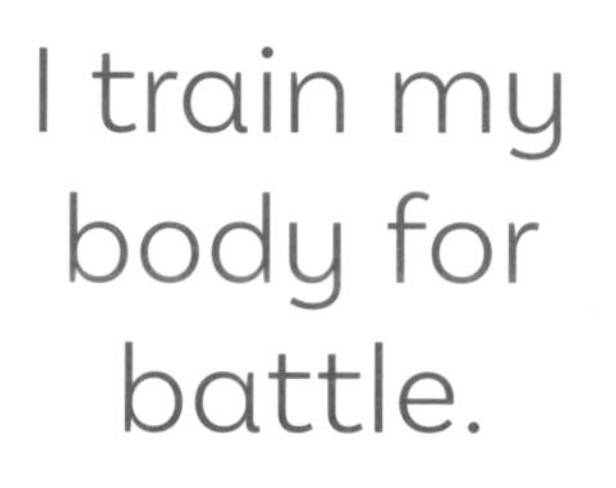

I train my
body for
battle.

And I train my mind
for battle, too.

I fill my heart with kindness,
the most powerful
weapon there is.

I am a leader of the strong

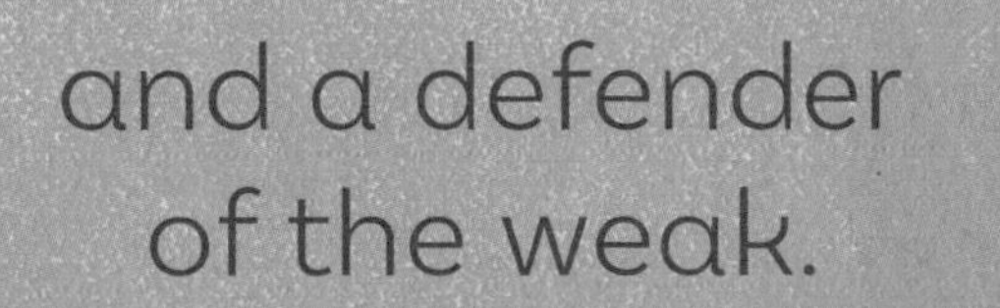

and a defender
of the weak.

I am grateful.

I am generous.

I am fierce.

I am loving.

I belong to a family of warriors.
And my family belongs to the earth.

At the end of each day,
I say goodnight
to the sun

and the earth

and the wind.

Even warrior goddesses
go to sleep.

For my mother,
who fought
every battle
with kindness.

J.A.

This book was inspired by *Warrior Goddess Training* by HeatherAsh Amara.
Visit her website at heatherashamara.com and Hierophant at hierophantpublishing.com to learn more.

Sounds True
Boulder, CO 80306

Published 2018

Book design by Beth Skelley
Printed in South Korea

Library of Congress Cataloging-in-Publication Data
Names: Adams, Jennifer, 1970– author. | Lemniscates, Carme, illustrator.
Title: I am a warrior goddess / by Jennifer Adams ; illustrations by Carme Lemniscates.
Description: Boulder, CO : Sounds True, [2018] | Audience: Age: 4–8. | Audience: K to Grade 3.
Identifiers: LCCN 2017019563 (print) | LCCN 2017045778 (ebook) | ISBN 9781683640462 (ebook) | ISBN 9781683640059 (hardcover)
Subjects: LCSH: Self-reliance—Juvenile literature. | Self-confidence—Juvenile literature.
Classification: LCC BJ1533.S27 (ebook) | LCC BJ1533.S27 A33 2018 (print) | DDC 155.43/3—dc23
LC record available at https://lccn.loc.gov/2017019563

10 9 8 7 6 5 4 3 2 1